HARD BODIES

JUSTIN GRIMBOL

ATLATL

ISBN-10: 1941918042
ISBN-13: 978-1-941918-04-3

Published by:
Atlatl Press
POB 222
Yellow Springs, Ohio 45387

HARD BODIES

For Heather

THE BINGO SORCERESS

"Are you wearing a sweat suit?" Bella asked.

"Maybe," I said.

I was in the kitchen scavenging for crackers. And yes, I was wearing a black sweatshirt and black sweat pants. It was a sweat suit. It's true.

"You are wearing a sweat suit," she said. "And it's the creepiest, cutest sweat suit ever. Have you left the house yet today?"

Bella was my wife and she had just come home from work and she looked happy to see me, regardless of the sweat suit and my freaked-out cave dweller appearance.

She even gave me a hug.

"I love you," she said.

"You're hugging me too tightly," I said.

She let go and rolled her eyes.

1

"So, what did you do today?" she asked.

"I worked on stuff."

"Like what?"

"Writing stuff."

"What kinda writing stuff?"

"Just stuff."

I looked at the light in the kitchen.

"Have you been in the house all day?" she asked.

I looked at her face. I loved that face. I loved her big eyes and her dirty blond hair and her goofy expressions.

I stared at her face awhile.

"Wow. You are really out of it," she said.

"I'm so out of it right now. I haven't left the house all day and I feel cray-cray."

She laughed. Bella loved the term "cray-cray."

And I usually loved Bella's bouncy laughter. But it was too much for me right then.

"You don't get it. I feel like shit. I wanted to ride my bike, but there was too much snow and ice. It's a snowpocalypse out there."

Bella laughed. She also loved the term "snowpocalypse." She thought she had invented it, but I was the one who had invented it.

"I invented that word," she said.

"Can we please not fight right now? I've had a rough day."

"You've had a rough day! I had a doozy of a day," Bella said.

She started listing all the things that happened at work. She worked as a recreational coordinator at a neurological center. She worked with the kids. They had a variety of issues. Some couldn't talk or even move much. Most of them had behavioral issues. Biting and head butting was normal. So was poop-throwing. One kid liked to swallow shoes. That's right, whole shoes.

Earlier that day, she had asked this one kid to go to bed. He called her a fat bitch. He wanted to stay up eating cookies and watching TV. That was understandable enough. Bella suggested a compromise. Maybe he could have one more cookie and maybe even a chocolate milk, but he had to go to bed. "Fuck your compromise, fat bitch," the kid said. Then as she was walking down the hall she saw the kid's little middle fingers poking in and out of his room.

"And then there's this one kid," she went on. "He calls me Hairy Armpits. And now all the kids call me Hairy Armpits."

I smiled. I liked that nickname. It was a good nickname.

She had hairy armpits because of me. I thought they were sexy. When we first started dating, I asked her to grow her armpit hair out and she agreed.

Bella kept listing off crazed things the kids in her program had done.

But it all sounded adorable to me. And I could tell she wasn't really bothered by it either.

Her last job was much rougher.

The kids threw poop at her almost every other day and she

got head-butted frequently.

One time a kid dug a bunch of poop out of his butthole and grabbed her hair. It took five men to pry the kid off her. She lost a bunch of hair and smelled poopy for days.

This new job was easy by comparison. And she knew that.

Still, she liked to bitch.

"You need to cut your hair," she said, switching subjects.

"What? No," I said. "I want my hair to be long and powerful."

"Honey, you're balding. When you have long hair you just look creepy. Plus you need to start looking for a job."

"I know. You're right."

"What do you want for dinner?" she asked.

"Let's skip dinner and go to Bingo night," I said.

"Should we?"

"Fuck it, we've both had rough days. You got called out on your hairy arm pits and I had my wife call me a creepy bald guy."

She nodded.

"Do we have the money?"

"We'll take some out of our savings."

She got excited and started hopping around the house, clapping her hands and making weird noises.

I loved it when Bella got excited like that.

I loved watching her.

She was so goofy. So goofy it went right past clumsy and awkward and became something beautiful.

And she had a good laugh. It was loud and sloppy. It took guts to have a laugh like that.

Guts and a big butt. My wife had a big butt. A big, warm butt. A stinky butt. I was sure that big butt was linked to her laugh somehow. The secret to that laugh was in there. I just had to find it. With my face.

"Look at my butt!" she said, as she was changing out of her work clothes. "It's my butt. Not yours."

I grabbed it. And squeezed.

She slapped my hand away and ran off, laughing.

We drove to the Ivanhoe, this cozy Irish pub on Main Street in Racine.

There was barely anybody there. I figured it was going to be easy to win.

We ordered dark, dark stouts and some bingo cards.

The girl reading the numbers was drunk and acting belligerent and wild and that wildness made all the unfunny things she said hilarious and, even though she had a weak chin and no hips and tacky highlights in her hair, I wanted to cuddle with her and smell her butt a little.

But I held my wifey close, hoping she could protect my chubby body against this bingo sorceress and her boozy magic.

"O 69," she called out.

And everyone laughed.

Things got rowdy.

I got rowdy.

Every time I got a number I hooted and hollered and acted nuts.

But, even though there were only six people in the bar, I didn't win a single game.

I got drunk.

Some old guy bought us shots.

There was a muscle bound middle-age dude at the bar. He grabbed Bella's butt when she walked to the bathroom.

I looked at him. It wasn't a mean look. Or an angry look. Just a look.

I was thinking, *Man, this guy looks like a gym teacher.*

The guy caught me staring.

At first I thought he was going to fight me, but then he apologized for grabbing my wife's ass. And bought me a beer.

I drank the beer.

Bella came back.

The guy bought her a beer as well.

Bella laughed and rolled her eyes.

Bella, the old ass grabber, and I raised our glasses and made a toast.

"BUTTS ARE AWESOME!" I yelled.

Bella cheered.

We kissed.

Her kiss tasted like warmth.

CAVEMAN UNTHAWED

I drove to the Best Buy on Route 31.

It had been five years since I had bought a new computer and I was not prepared for how futuristic things had gotten.

Shopping in Best Buy was like being in *Back to The Future Part II*.

I didn't know what was going on.

This nerd lady showed me a computer with a touch screen.

"Oh I don't need anything that fancy," I told her.

She looked confused.

"They all have touch screens," she said.

"Really," I said.

She nodded.

"Even the super cheap ones?"

She nodded again.

"Wow," I said.

I browsed around.

All the computers looked weird. The mouse pads were too big and the keyboards were tiny and the letters lit up and made them look way too spaceshippy for me.

Maybe if I was an alien with four eyes and six dicks I could get used to a keyboard that bright. But my human eyes were too human and it hurt just looking at such super futuristic space age computers. My one human-sized dick felt inadequate.

And all the keyboards looked that way now. The nerd assured me of this.

I didn't like this.

I wanted to run away and hide and write with a quill pen for the rest of my career.

That wasn't really an option though.

I had to get a computer.

I started confiding in the nerd. I told her about my last computer, how it was only two hundred bucks.

"They told me it would only work for a couple years," I said.

The nerd lady nodded.

"But it still works. That fucking thing's still running. It just won't die."

The nerd laughed. She liked this story.

At this point I had found my machine. I was looking it over, playing with its keyboard, when I noticed it didn't have a DVD player.

"Holy shit," I said. "Where's the DVD player?"

She looked confused.

"You mean the optical port?"

"Woah," I said.

She laughed.

She explained to me that most laptops don't have an optical port these days.

"Then how the fuck do you watch DVDs?"

"You download them. You stream them from Netflix or Hulu."

"But I don't have the internet."

"Who doesn't have the internet?"

"Me," I said. "I don't. Shit's expensive."

"It's like twenty bucks a month."

"Expensive."

She showed me an external DVD player I could use. It was cheap enough. I told her I wanted that too.

My wife was really impressed by the new computer.

"It's so futuristic," she kept saying.

"I know," I said. "It's like we're in *The Jetsons*."

"What the fuck is *The Jetsons*?" she asked.

"It's a show. You've never seen *The Jetsons*? Wow. I forget how young you are."

"Yeah, 'cause I'm so much more responsible and level-headed than you."

"Well, I wouldn't put it that way," I said.

I started playing with my new computer.

Bella watched for a while but then got bored.

By the time I was done my wife was asleep.

I shut the blinds to my apartment. Let the place become drafty with winter air, like an old-timey castle.

I disrobed and walked around my apartment in the nude.

My penis peeked over my gut and looked up at me. It was so full of mischief. Such a rascal.

I got the lube and the glow in the dark pocket pussy my wife had given me for my birthday.

I sat in my favorite chair in the living room.

I played with my cock and my balls until I was hard.

I put some lube on it. Just a little. Not too much.

The pocket pussy glowed. It looked like a chubby, radioactive worm.

I put my dick in it. I put my dick in and out of it.

I felt like I was a making love to an alien.

SIR TEXTS-A-LOT

Weather.com said that Racine was going to get up to six inches of snow.

But they were wrong. We got twelve inches.

And for most of the day I felt cozy hiding away in my apartment.

Then I realized I hadn't left the apartment much in the past couple days. Staying in started to seem less glamorous.

I got stir crazy.

And started texting people.

One of the people I texted was Rhoda, an old college friend.

Sometimes I sent her stuff to edit. She had edited my last book, *The Party Lords*. It was unreal how thorough her edits were. I had sent her a book to edit a few months before and I hadn't gotten it back.

So I texted her asking about the book.

The day moped along.

Snow piled up outside.

Hours passed.

It got dark.

Rhoda still hadn't responded to my texts.

I got nervous.

She used to love my wacky hijinks back in college. Like when I threw Q-tips all over her room and rubbed deodorant on her bed spread. Or the time I wore her special sexy underpants and left a skid mark on them. We had some fun times together.

But maybe she had grown up. Maybe she had grown up and decided she had no time for my shenanigans.

The thought of this made me sad and lonely hearted.

I texted her again. *YO LETS PHONE CHAT!* I wrote. *I got fascinating stuff to say!!!!!!*

No response.

I paced my apartment.

Who was going to proofread my manuscripts?

Who would fill me in on gossip of celebrities and old classmates?

These things were important to me.

I texted her again. This time my message was more random.

I GOT EXTRA ARM PIT HAIR, I wrote.

Then I wrote: *That's not true. I don't have much arm pit hair.*

I made sure the texts were as random as possible. I didn't want to seem too needy.

I waited.

I watched a rom com I had rented from Redbox..

An hour or so passed.

The rom com wasn't very romantic or funny.

I checked my phone.

Still, no response.

What the fuck? What had I done to upset my friend like this?

Maybe she was tired of me making fun of her clothing. She had bought that expensive sweater with the deer patterns on it and I had told her she looked like a Christmas ornament. But that was over seven years ago.

Could she still be mad about that?

I texted her again. *I'm going to keep texting you nonsense until you respond,* I wrote.

I waited.

Nothing.

I only have two nipples, I wrote. *Discuss.*

Then I wrote. *Did you know I'm a bass guitarist? Cause it's true.*

Then I wrote. *Have you ever heard of Stephen King? Rumor has it the motherfucker writes books.*

Then I wrote. *I own an internet.*

I waited. It was now ten at night and she still hadn't responded. I was feeling anxious.

I had done so many offensive things to this girl.

I had gotten drunk and force kissed her like a dozen times.

I once punched her in the arm really hard and then called her a dork and then she cried. And we weren't kids when I did this. I was like twenty-five.

I once ruined her birthday party by starting a food fight and then having group sex with her best friend and my wife. I came all over her couch.

I decided to text her again.

Have you ever seen the movie Dances with Wolverine?

I laughed. I liked the idea of Hugh Jackman and Kevin Costner dancing.

How could she ignore such a hilarious text?

Then I wrote. *Hey, are you doing this on purpose? Are you ignoring me just so I keep sending you such hilarious texts?*

The idea of her doing this made me really mad because she knew how sensitive I could be. She knew I had anxiety issues.

Pull yourself together, I thought. You're being needy.

My wife asked me what I was doing.

I told her about my situation with Rhoda.

"I'm sure she's just asleep," she said. "Call her in the morning."

I smiled and nodded.

But there was no way I could do that.

I needed resolution.

I sent some more random texts.

I invented a new kind of bubble gum. Here's the secret ingredient.

HARD BODIES

I've read a book about outer space. True story.

I eat breakfast in the afternoon sometimes.

My wife called me to bed. She did look extra warm and cuddly. I got under the covers and we played around a little. Then I started to get anxious again.

"What if Rhoda doesn't want to be my friend anymore?" I asked

She laughed and told me I was being crazy and she kissed my forehead.

I became drowsy.

Shortly afterward I was able to pass out.

But my peace of mind was short lived.

I woke up at four in the morning.

Looked at my phone.

Rhoda still hadn't texted back.

Damn.

I texted her.

Hey. You. I woke up early. I had a dream that I was a rich girl and that I had this weird disease that only rich girls get and it made my pinky itch and then I woke up and my pinky was still itchy. I think a spider bit it.

I waited and watched the sun come up.

How cold hearted could she be?

Finally I snapped.

Rhoda please respond. Are you ok?

Just so I didn't sound too needy I attached a picture of my

nipple to the message.

My phone rang.

It was Rhoda.

I answered.

"Are you mad at me?"

She laughed.

"No, I just lost my phone while going Christmas tree shopping."

"Oh…"

"These are some really funny texts," she said.

"Thanks."

We chatted for a while.

I asked her to gossip but she didn't know any.

She had a job.

She'd been busy.

Too busy to learn any new gossip.

That made me sad. Rhoda was the queen of gossip. She was the champagne of gossip, while most just served up box wine.

But she had no more. Nothing new, at least. She had been too busy.

I knew some gossip though. I didn't have a job and I had more than enough time to spy on some of our friends on Facebook and I was more than glad to fill her in on what they were doing.

SOMEWHERE WARM

I woke up and kissed Bella's warm body.

She opened her eyes. Looked at me.

"Ten more minutes," she said.

I rolled over.

She curled up behind me. That's how we did it. She was the big spoon. I was the little spoon. Even though, technically, I was a much bigger spoon.

I felt safe with her behind me like that. But I also felt like I had to fart. I had never been very good at self-control so I released the Kraken.

"Gross! Did you just fart onto my cooter?" Bella asked.

"I just gave you my fart. It's your fart now. Do what you will with it."

She laughed.

Then went back to sleep.

ROM COMS

I ran around our apartment naked.

My fat body made me feel extra naked. Like I had more private parts than most people.

My wife was in the living room cleaning something.

I ran around her and then out of the room and then I ran back in the room, and then I flexed my muscles and growled at her.

She hugged me and my dick rubbed against her sweat pants and it felt good.

But then I decided I didn't want to have sex. Not yet, at least.

"Get away from me," I yelled. "I have to shower."

I pushed her away.

Then I ran to the bathroom.

I got in the shower and let the hot water run over me.

I rubbed the bar of soap over my man boobs and my gut until I was all sudsy.

I shampooed my hair and then I was done.

I walked out of the shower and looked for clothes.

"It's ten degrees outside," Bella yelled to me. "Negative for real-feel."

I laughed. She loved the term real-feel.

There was a pile of clothes in my closet. I searched through it.

I found a pair of sweat pants and some almost clean socks and a pretty cool looking shirt.

And I found a dildo. A medium sized, flesh colored dildo, with a suction cup at the base.

A few years ago I had ordered this dildo off Amazon.com. It wasn't for my wife. It was for me. But it was too big and I couldn't fit it in my butt. So I gave it to my wife and she used it every once in a while.

"HEY BABY!" I yelled. "Come here!"

She didn't respond.

"BABY, GET OVER HERE!" I kept yelling.

"Hold your horses," she yelled back.

I heard her walk through the living room, then the dining room.

"Your aunt keeps calling. I think she wants to make plans for Christmas. So annoying."

She got closer.

I could hear her in the kitchen now.

I waited until I could see her shadow. Then I threw the dildo at the door to our room.

It flew right by her.

It slammed into the door and made a loud bang.

She screamed.

"WHAT THE FUCK!" she yelled.

I ran over and looked at her. She had spilt coffee all over herself.

She looked at me.

Then she looked at the dildo.

We both started laughing.

"That was so fucked up," she said.

I kept laughing.

She got into bed.

I got in with her.

But I didn't want to have sex. I just wanted to be lazy. Cuddle. Smell her crotch a little.

"We should watch a rom com later," she said.

"That sounds nice," I said.

REAL-FEEL TEMP

I had a dream about this grumpy Greek girl I had dated back in high school.

In this dream her skin was soft gold and her lips were painted blue.

She let me touch her boobs a little. That was nice.

Then I woke up.

I spent most of the morning sitting in bed naked and feeling sappy and thinking about the dream.

I started analyzing it.

I liked analyzing dreams. I got really new agey when it came to dreams. Still do.

So I lay in bed. And I thought about the dream like it was some sort of secret code.

I decided the Greek ex-girlfriend represented death. Not in an ugly way. But in a spooky, beautiful way.

It made my soul feel soggy and heavy and boner-ridden.

Why would she represent death?

Well, she took my virginity and then my mom died a week later. We dated for a short time. Like six months or so.

We fought a lot and did weird sex stuff. I ate her butt. Her butt was the first butt I had ever licked. She had turned me into a butt licker, and for that, I am eternally grateful.

Usually I keep in touch with my ex-girlfriends. But not the Greek.

I had run into her a few times since we broke up, but we had never really stayed in touch. The last time I saw her was a long, long time ago.

She lived in a much more untouchable part of my past.

Thinking about her made me feel sappy and feeling sappy in this way was no good. I was already too nostalgic and any-thing that made me feel any more nostalgia than usual was dangerous.

I had to shake this.

I walked down to the coffee shop.

I got some coffee then found a table and set up my laptop.

The internet connection was fast.

And the coffee was strong. Too strong. I felt like I had just snorted a line of cocaine.

I tried to find my ex on Facebook and Twitter. But she wasn't on Facebook or Twitter.

I felt discouraged.

And overly caffeinated.

I messaged my buddy Mike. I told him about the dream.

He wrote back, *When you die she's going to fold you gently into her giant maternal womb and keep you safe there, forever safe from everything except for her. She's going to yell at you. A lot.*

I liked that idea. It kinda turned me on.

But he wasn't getting it. It wasn't ugly. It was sweet. Or as sweet as death could be.

I kept trying to talk about the dream.

He seemed bored.

He changed the subject.

How was your step-mom's funeral, he wrote.

I told him it was *beautiful. The hymns ripped me apart. I cried a lot. Hymns do that to me.*

I waited for him to respond.

It was taking way too long. I got bored and checked my email.

There was a mass email from my father's church. A family friend, Pastor Walter, had just passed.

I was taken aback.

How strange that I would dream of death and then get this email the next day.

I called my dad. Told him about Walter.

I listened to him sigh over the phone.

Then I told him I loved him.

I walked down the street to a shitty diner and ate an omelet. It had lots of chopped up vegetables and American cheese in it.

As I ate, I thought about my old home back in Sag Harbor, New York. My cousin Carl had just bought it from my father. I had visited recently and my old house was all fixed up and fancy looking.

Carl let me search around the basement.

I found old comics I had drawn and notebooks full of heavy metal lyrics my good friend Jay had written when he was nineteen and living with me.

It made me laugh.

The lyrics were hysterical.

"Increasingly morbid are these goblinoid beasts in which I coexist with!"

I liked the word "goblinoid."

I sang these lyrics to myself as I searched through more old crap.

And I found a box of tapes. They were recordings of my mother preaching.

I finished my omelet and went back to my apartment and looked at my mother's tapes.

I used to hate those tapes because it reminded me that my mother was very dead and that, when she was alive, her voice was high pitched, like Roseanne Barr, not the deep, soothing angelic voice I remembered her having.

But now I felt ready to listen to the tapes. To hear her real voice again.

So I spent the rest of the afternoon searching around Racine for a tape player.

I checked out all the nearby thrift shops. They didn't have one.

I went online.

I wrote to Mike. *I got a whole box of the shit. And death visiting me as a sexy ex-girlfriend in my dreams. And I got a book full of heavy metal lyrics Gorcoff wrote when he was nineteen. I can't find a fucking tape player. I just need a tape player.*

Just take it in slowly, Mike wrote back.

What a weird response.

Was I freaking my old buddy out?

Shit.

I apologized to him for sounding crazy.

I waited for him to write back and got bored again.

I prowled Facebook some more.

There were many posts about Pastor Walter. Many sweet posts. Filled with love. Filled with appreciation. All heavily marinated with a sense of loss.

I started to write something about Pastor Walter, but then I remembered I didn't know him very well.

Instead, I wrote to a bunch of friends on Facebook asking them about my ex and if they had heard from her.

While I waited for a response, my wifey called.

She was still at work. She sounded stressed.

"What's wrong?" I asked.

"Nothing. I took the kids to that indoor water park today.

This one kid has Huntington's and he can't walk so I carried him up the slides all day and I'm physically just worn the fuck out. What are you up to?"

"Nothing. Hunting the reaper. Or my ex-girlfriend's ghost. Why?"

There was a pause. I could imagine how tired and confused and annoyed she must look on the other end of the line.

"Okay," she said. "What else are you doing today?"

"Nothing. Gotta go. Busy."

She told me she loved me and I told her the same and then hung up the phone.

I looked at my laptop.

Went to Amazon.com. There were no new reviews of my book.

I went back onto Facebook.

One of my old high school friends had responded. He said he hadn't seen or heard from my ex.

Then he wrote, *Remember how you could lift your balls up and down without using your hands. You called it The Elevator. You would show it to people all the time. You would even take girls in the bathroom and show it to them.*

I laughed.

What a good memory.

I was starting to feel less fucked up.

The image of my golden ex-grirlfriend was still there and I was still over-caffeinated and feeling way too soulful and magical. Death was still stalking me. Or at least playing a weird game of ring and run with my soul. But I also felt a little livelier, a little more in the present. And that was good.

I decided to not finish my third cup of coffee.

I needed to be outside.

It was brutally cold.

The internet said the real-feel temp was negative five.

I didn't care.

I just wanted to feel the daylight.

GOBLINOID JELL-O SHOTS

It was late and I had Jell-O shots all over me.

"Your beard is so red," my wife kept saying.

"Whatever," I said. "I like it that way."

I licked my beard. It tasted like cherry.

I licked it some more. So good.

I had some on my jacket and on my collar. It tasted so good.

I ordered more Jell-O shots. This time I chose the color purple. It tasted so purple.

My buddy Ron and I were feeling mischievous.

We wanted to pull a little prank on the bar. We put ten bucks in the jukebox and then picked "Beat It" by Michael Jackson and set it up to play ten times in a row.

The song turned on and we giggled like little kids.

Some of the women in the bar started dancing.

"They're getting into it now, but once it plays a few times in a row, it'll start to drive them nuts," I said.

"We should put more money in the machine," Ron said. "We can have this song playing all night."

"It's a genius plan."

As we were walking to the jukebox another song turned on. It wasn't "Beat It." It was some Kid Rock song.

What the fuck had happened?

"Beat It" was supposed to be playing. It was supposed to be playing ten times in a row.

We were confused.

Did the machine somehow know what we were up to?

Maybe we weren't allowed to play the same song twice in a row.

We tried again. We put ten bucks into the machine and this time we played "Beat It" every other song.

We waited.

"Beat It" wouldn't turn on.

"We've been had," I said.

"I just don't get it," Ron said.

"The machine outsmarted us."

The local roller derby team was at the bar celebrating their first game or match or bout, whatever they call it.

There was this one chick who made my heart flutter.

She gave me a boner. Not just physically, but emotionally.

Her body was curvy. She had a potbelly and a big ass.

She wore a tight fitting sweatshirt that had red and green stripes and it reminded me of Freddy Krueger, if he was female and not all burnt up.

"That girl's body makes me emotional," I said.

Ron nodded. He wasn't as into it.

He was still thinking about the jukebox. I could tell.

"Seriously, look at that body. I got so many boners right now. Spiritually, I mean."

He looked at her.

"She's wearing a nice Freddy Krueger sweatshirt," he said.

"I agree."

I kept staring at the girl. I had a bit of a staring problem.

My wife and Ron's fiancé were dancing together. There was a guy on the other side of the bar staring at them.

"Is that what I look like when I stare at chicks?" I asked Ron.

He laughed.

Eventually the Freddy Krueger chick caught me staring at her.

She walked up to me.

She mumbled something.

She wanted to dance.

"I don't trust you," I said. "What if this is a dream and you stab me with your knife fingers and then I die in real life as well? You know. 'Cause you look like Freddy Krueger."

She mumbled something else. She was starting to sound

more annoyed than flirtatious.

"You do have a really nice stomach though," I said.

She stumbled off and I looked at Ron.

"That girl just flirted with me," I said.

He nodded.

"It doesn't take much to make me feel manly," I said.

"I hear ya," he said.

My wife and his fiancé walked over.

"I saw that girl hit on you," Bella said.

"I think she liked my body," I said.

"I'm so proud of you," she said.

We ordered more Jell-O shots.

"I want to meet the chef that made these Jell-O shots," I said.

My wife laughed. "You have so much red Jell-O in your beard."

I ordered another round.

We raised our little Jell-O shots in the air.

"TO FREDDY KRUEGER CHICK!" I yelled.

We took our shots.

A homeless guy stumbled into the bar.

I gave him some change.

He smiled at me.

Then he left the bar.

I ordered another round of Jell-O shots.

I was drunk.

I was a little too drunk.

"I wish they had some non-alcoholic Jell-O shots," I said.

Everyone looked confused.

An hour or so later, the homeless guy came back into the bar and asked me for change.

"I already gave you change," I said.

He got mad and mumbled some angry things at me.

I reached into my pocket and found a dime and some pennies. I gave it to him.

He walked out of the bar and into the cold slippery night.

THE HISTORY OF
OUR CHRISTMAS CARDS

Bella wanted to work on our Christmas cards.

I groaned.

She had started this obnoxious ritual two years before.

At first, I thought it would be funny. I had found this picture on the internet I thought we should use. It was of an older guy with graying hair holding his smiling teenage girlfriend while pointing a gun at the camera. I thought it would be the best Christmas card ever.

Bella disagreed.

We fought about it for a while.

I felt like she was trying to domesticate me.

We argued until we both felt ridiculous and stubborn and then, finally, we came to a compromise. We found a picture of us on Facebook. It was a bad picture. We both looked grumpy as hell.

After printing the pictures at Walgreens, we let the cards sit in a stack for a while.

"We should really send these cards out," we kept saying.

Christmas came and went and we never sent the cards out.

The next year she wanted us to pose for another Christmas picture.

I still wanted to use the picture of the old dude with the gun and his teenage girlfriend. It reminded me of The Virgin Mary and Joseph and I thought it embodied the Christmas Spirit.

She was really annoyed about that. She didn't like that picture.

"It's fucking creepy," she kept saying. "People are going to think this is our way of saying we're pregnant."

"That's hilarious," I said.

"No," she said. "It's not."

As a compromise I said I would pose for a new picture but she had to let me orchestrate the whole fucking thing.

She agreed.

In the end, it was another picture of us looking grumpy, but this time we were covered in a blanket and had our Christmas tree in the background.

Bella enjoyed setting up the shot. It felt festive to her. And I enjoyed looking grumpy.

Now it was that time of year again and she wanted me to set

up another picture.

First, I recommended us using the picture of my favorite old man and teenager.

"No, that's not acceptable," she said.

"One day you'll see the light," I said. "And we will finally use that awesome picture. Until then, I will keep it saved on my laptop. Digitally stored in the nether realm of my computer's brain chip."

She looked confused. She didn't know what a brain chip was. Neither did I.

I started coming up with ideas.

There were these two little ornamental birds in my dad's living room. They were pudgy and sleepy looking. Kinda like us.

Here was my brilliant idea. I was going to have Bella and me looking grumpy as usual. And we would be holding out the birds, like they were our special little Christmas souls.

I told Bella the idea and she loved it.

We drove to my father's apartment.

He was in his room, painting.

First I got him his coffee.

Then I set up the photo.

We sat in front of the TV and held the birds.

The camera timer was set. Bella pressed the button.

We watched the orange light blink.

The camera flashed.

I grabbed it and looked at our picture.

"What the fuck is with that face you're making?" I asked Bella.

"I think I look nice," she said.

"This is supposed to be a funny picture. Stop making that boring girl face."

"What boring girl face? You mean smiling?"

"You look insane. What kinda Martha Stewart bullshit face is that?"

"Fuck you."

"Is this really what I married? I thought I married this rambunctious crazy ass goofy-as-fuck girl. Every year you act more and more like the shitty rich girlfriends you grew up with."

"I do not! And if you're going to be a dick, then I'm done with that picture."

She got up and walked over to the couch to pout.

I thought about the picture with the old guy and his young pregnant girlfriend. Or maybe it was his wife. Who could tell?

I looked over at Bella. She was so pissed.

I crawled over to her and apologized for having weird anger management issues.

She liked hearing apologies. All I ever had to do was say "I'm sorry" and she cheered up instantly.

"Can you please make a funny face for the picture?" I asked.

She nodded.

I told her I was sorry again.

She smiled.

I loved that smile. I really loved it. It inspired me. It made me think of great things.

I decided to elaborate on the pic.

I wanted to get my dad in on it.

He was already wearing a big green nightgown at three in the afternoon and nothing, I mean nothing, sings the sweet song of Christmas cheer like wearing a nightgown in the middle of the day.

My father and I held the two little fat birds and Bella held a little statue of a penguin.

We posed for the picture and they were both smiling like they were getting their school picture taken.

I got mad again.

"Stop fucking SMILING!" I yelled.

We took the next picture.

In this one my dad looked like he was about to cry and Bella looked angry. My face just looked goofy and aloof. It was perfect.

"Send this motherfucker to the printers, sweetie. We got us the perfect Christmas card."

She looked at the pic and laughed.

"It is kinda cute," she said.

"As long as Bella likes it, I like it," my father said.

I looked at the picture.

"I'm a goddamned artsy-fartsy genius," I said.

Bella kissed me.

"You're adorable like a fucking half-penguin, half-bear," she said.

I didn't want to be adorable. I wanted to be sexy and manly like Channing Tatum.

But I figured, fuck it. A half-penguin, half-bear was pretty badass too.

OVERWEIGHT, POORLY DRESSED CHANNING TATUM LOOKALIKE MEETS HIPPO SANTA

There was a package on our front porch.

The package said it was for Bella and Eddie Grimbol.

The word FRAGILE was marked on the edge, so I opened it carefully.

There were three pairs of socks and a picture frame.

Fragile? I thought. Seriously?

I searched through the package and found a letter at the bottom.

I opened it.

The letter was from Bella's mom, Hilary.

Oh fuck, I thought. Bella's mom got her fucking socks for Christmas.

This was the lamest present a parent could get their kid.

Hilary was a champion of parental awkwardness. She was also a demonoid Mainer, fueled by all things passive aggressive. So I wasn't really surprised by the box of Christmas socks, but my heart still ached for Bella.

I called my father and told him about the box of socks.

He was appalled and heart achy for Bella as well.

"What are you going to do?" he asked. "Should we take her out to dinner?"

Dinner was his answer to all things sad and painful.

But this was going to take more than fancy dining.

"There's only one thing I can do," I said.

I got dressed. I got in my Jeep and drove to the Goodwill.

The place was packed.

I grabbed a cart and pushed my way to the back of the store where the Christmas decorations were kept.

They had lots of good stuff.

I found an ornament hippo dressed up as Santa. A hippo Santa. I had never seen a hippo Santa before. It seemed like an obvious animal to turn into a Santa, but it had never been done. I was excited. AND IT WAS ONLY 2.99!

I grabbed that and a bunch of candles and other tacky Christmas decorations.

I bought her some cookbooks and random kitchen shit.

Then I rushed to the counter.

The woman behind the counter was large and friendly looking. Except for the growth on her face. It was the size of candy corn. But it was pink. Very pink.

I wanted to touch it. But I didn't.

I didn't touch it.

She caught me staring though. She could tell I wanted to touch her growth. I think I made her nervous.

"Fifty dollars and six cents," she said.

"Holy shit," I said.

I passed her my debit card.

I wasn't sure Bella and I even had any money in the account. But I gave her the card anyway. It went through.

Fuck, I thought. Bella is going to be so pissed. This really backfired.

I drove home and set up the decorations.

I hid the presents in the back of my jeep.

Bella came home at eight.

She was exhausted.

As soon as she opened the door, I hugged her and kissed her and sniffed her and grabbed her butt.

She laughed.

She told me about her day.

A kid had swallowed a light bulb and had to get sent to the emergency room.

"How's that even possible?" she kept saying.

I didn't know what to tell her.

Then she saw the package her mom had sent.

She opened it.

I was expecting her to get teary-eyed, confused, hurt. I was expecting rage. I was expecting deep sadness.

I was sure all the sadness from having a shitty mom would erupt and ghostly shrapnel from her soul would fly around our apartment.

I watched her open the package.

Part of me wanted to jump at her and yell "DON'T DO IT!" and tackle her and hold her and tell her I loved her and her body and her big warm butt.

But I didn't.

I sat there. I watched her open the package.

She held the socks up.

"Oh cool, I needed new socks."

"You like the socks?" I asked.

"Yeah, they look really warm."

Then she noticed the decorations.

"What a nice thing to come home to," she said.

She noticed the hippo Santa and laughed.

"The house looks great," she said.

"I thought your mom's shitty presents would upset you, so I got you a bunch of shit to cheer you up," I said.

She liked that. It made her laugh.

It was the biggest goofiest laugh.

She jumped on my lap.

I held her.

And I could smell her vagina a little.

I wanted to have sex.

But my phone rang.

I answered.

It was my dad.

He had computer problems.

I told Bella I had to go. I had to help my father.

She kissed me and I left.

Before I got to my father's, I stopped at a gas station and bought a Diet Raspberry Snapple.

There was a long line in front of the register.

I stood there and got bored and tired and lonely.

I wanted to be at home with Bella.

I wanted to smell her vagina and her butt cheeks.

I also wanted to smell under her big boobs. The under-boob. That's a really nice damp area of the female body that isn't given enough credit.

Finally, I bought my Snapple and drove to my father's.

He sat on his La-Z-Boy wearing a skimpy nightgown, balls exposed.

I asked him what was wrong with his computer.

"Nothing," he said.

"Then why did you call me over here?"

"Well, I thought something was wrong with my computer but then there was nothing wrong with it and it worked fine."

He asked me for a diet soda in a glass filled with ice.

Then I watched some TV with him.

Then I went home.

Bella was still there.

She was cleaning the kitchen.

I felt bad. She always had to clean up after me.
I had let a massive amount of dishes pile up.
I was bad at doing the dishes.

HIPPO SANTA IS NOT LUTHERAN, BUT HE DOES HANG OUT WITH LUTHERANS SOMETIMES

My buddy Jay visited us for the holidays.

He took the train all the way from the middle of Bum-Fuck Pennsylvania where he taught art at a small college and rode that thing all the way to Racine. It was a thirty-hour ride.

When I picked him up from the train station he looked fully alert and unfazed by the journey though. His curly hair was up in a bun. And his face had just the right amount of scruff. The guy looked handsome.

We hugged then got in my warm Jeep.

"It was a good ride," he said. "Nearly lost my mind though. The seats on the train were so hard. So uncomfortable. And I'm pretty sure the guy I was sitting next to was a serial killer. He had that look in his eyes. Well, he slept most of the way so I didn't really see his eyes much, but you know what I mean."

"That's awesome," I said.

"He smelled like pepperonis," he said. "I usually don't mind dry meats. They are healthier for you. Can't handle when a man smells that way though."

"That makes sense."

The wind picked up.

Jay zippered his jacket.

"Jesus fuck, Wisconsin is basically the arctic," he said.

"I know," I said. "It's been rough."

"Fucking world's ending, bro."

"I know."

"It's kinda exciting."

"It gives me anxiety," I said.

"Let's get something to eat," he said. "I'm fucking famished."

Then he gave me a big hug. A hard hug. It hurt a little. But I liked it.

I drove him to Asiana's.

We got some curry.

I told him about the plan for the night.

"I'm taking you to a Christmas party," I said. "Church ladies galore."

"I'm into that. Will there be food?"

"Lots."

"Will there be booze?"

"They will have wine. So much wine."

"I can't wait," he said.

We talked for a while, then drove back to my place and napped a little.

Bella got home around six.

She saw Jay and then hopped up and down and gave him a big hug.

"UNCLE JAY IS HERE!" she kept yelling.

There was some more hugging.

Then she broke away and started talking about work.

A kid had eaten his own diaper.

Jay looked visibly very nauseous. So I asked Bella to cease and desist.

Then we headed out.

The party was at Debby's place.

It was a cozy time.

There was cheese and wine.

Jay talked to a couple of ministers about old timey religious paintings.

Bella joked with the church ladies about how sloppy I was.

At one point we sat around the table with some church people and joked about the sloppiness of Christmas past.

"There was this one Christmas we really said fuck it to the whole family thing," I said.

"Is that the time you vomited all Christmas?" Jay asked with his arm around my neck.

"No, I mean the one where we just hung out in Montauk."

"THE DUNES!" he said. Getting excited. "THE FUCK-ING DUNES! THAT WAS AWESOME! We went for that long hike. You made me read shitty poetry out loud."

"Ginsberg. It was bad stuff. But I loved getting all new ag-ey on Christmas."

"You guys are such dorks," Bella said. "Who spends Christmas hiking on a beach?"

"It was awesome," Jay said.

"We got shot at," I said.

Everyone gasped.

"It was hunting season," I went on. "We kept hearing gun shots. I saw a bullet hit the sand near me."

"We had to hide behind this one dune," Jay said. "It was terrifying. It was awesome."

At one point we all sang carols. We all stood around the kitchen in a circle holding hands. I was drunk on wine and thought it was adorable.

As we sang, I looked over at Jay and started laughing. He looked so uncomfortable.

"Come on, Jay, give it some dry vocals," I said.

That's what we used to call the really tore up metal band vocals. Jay used to love dry vocals. "Love me some dry vo-cals," he used to say before howling out some verse from a metal song.

"Come on, Jay! Sing!"

He looked at me and shook his head. And his eyes said to me, "Please, bro, there is only so much of this I can take."

I laughed.

We stopped singing and started planning on getting to church.

I might have gotten a little too drunk on wine.

My wife and Jay also got too drunk. They were even drunker than I was and I'm pretty sure Bella said she was going to drive, even though she denied it.

"How the fuck are we going to get to church?" I asked Bella.

"Shit. I don't know. Why are you asking me?"

"Baby, I can't drive. I'm wasted."

"Well, I'm drunk too, so…"

I had to find us a ride.

All the other cars were already packed full of church ladies.

There was a group of young people in the living room and they looked sober. I didn't know who they were. Maybe kids or grandkids of all the church ladies.

I asked this one girl if she had a license and if she could drive my Jeep to church.

She looked annoyed.

"Come on. It's a brand new Jeep. It still smells nice. It has satellite radio. There's a porn channel. You can listen to the porn channel.”

"Gross," she said. "I don't wanna listen to that, but I will drive you to church if you're really all that shitfaced."

"Well, we aren't really shitfaced, just an itty bitty wee bitty too drunk to drive, that's all."

"Whatever," she said.

We all gathered in my Jeep.

The girl drove slowly.

"This is wild," Jay said. "We're full grown men and we have this teenage girl driving our drunk asses around."

"I know. Teenagers are awesome," I said.

We had glasses of wine from the party. We "cheers"ed with them.

"I'm not a fucking teenager," our driver said. "I'm twenty five."

There was an awkward silence.

"Teenagers are sensitive," Jay said.

We laughed and hooted and hollered and "cheers"ed again.

"I'M NOT A FUCKING TEENAGER!" our driver kept yelling.

"Hormones," I said.

"FUCK YOU!" she yelled.

"Stop being mean to the driver," Bella said.

"Sorry, Bella," Jay and I said.

I reached up front and turned on the porn channel.

A woman's voice seeped out of the speakers. It sounded so porny. I could practically smell the lube.

"So we're taking callers," she said.

Jay and I started giggling.

A man's voice came on. He sounded very southern.

"Uhh, hello," he said.

"Hello," the lady said. "You've reached Assy Ash. Would you like to tell us a good Christmasy fuck story?"

"I guess."

"Tell us, hon, you fuck anyone sexy this Christmas season?"

"Uhhh yeah."

"Who baby? Who did you fuck?"

"Uhh, well, I fucked your mom."

The Jeep was silent.

Was this really happening? Was someone prank calling the porn channel? ON CHRISTMAS EVE!

"I fucked your mom," the guy repeated.

The lady on the radio laughed nervously.

"So you fucked my mom?"

"Yup."

"How was it?"

"Well, she liked it alright, I do believe."

"Mmmm. That's sexy," she said.

Then she moved on to the next caller.

GLOW IN THE DARK
BABY JESUS

The church was lit by candles.

A mother and her daughter played violin.

I felt sappy.

It was a Lutheran church and much more traditional than I was used to or liked. But they did Christmas well and I was able to sustain that sappy feeling.

The thing I hated most about Lutheran church was communion. They have a communion fetish. They have it every Sunday. I found it to be exhausting.

"Are they going to do communion?" I asked an old lady who was sitting next to me."

"I don't know," she said.

"I hope not. It seems fucked up to celebrate his birth and crucifixion all at once. We should let him be a baby for a day before we sacrifice him and drink his blood."

I felt ashamed for being so snobby and gross with that old lady, but then she started laughing.

There ended up being communion. And the line leading up to the symbolic blood and body of Christ was really long and exhausting to look at.

"I can't believe this," I said to the old lady. "We just got done singing *hark the angels sing, glory to the newborn king* and now we are drinking his blood. That's morbid as hell."

She laughed again.

"Maybe they should have the loaf of bread shaped like the baby Jesus next time," she said.

"That's messed up," I said to the old lady.

We gave each other sneaky twisted smiles.

Then I got up there and took my communion.

Jay had never had communion before. He grabbed the goblet and took a big swig.

Bella looked at me with extra big eyes, pointed at Jay drinking from the goblet, and laughed.

"Was I not supposed to do that?" he asked me once we were seated.

I looked around. People were giving us dirty looks.

"It's fine," I told him.

My father gave his sermon.

I liked him up there, standing behind the pulpit, wearing his black robe. He looked as natural standing up there as he did on his La-Z-Boy, wearing his skimpy nightgown, balls hanging out.

Jay put his arm around my neck. He leaned in close. I could feel his stubble against my ear.

"Look at him, bro," he said. "He looks majestic up there."

I nodded. I smiled. I listened to my father's sermon.

He told us about when he went to camp and how afraid he was of the woods. And how that fear made him act bratty and horrible.

He told us about how the baby Jesus was supposed to offer light to the darkness.

Whoa, I thought. Baby Jesus is glow in the dark.

That thought seemed surprisingly stoned. I had not smoked in almost a year. But that was a really stoned idea. Super stoned. And I liked it. I liked thinking in a way that seemed stoned as hell, even though I hadn't smoked weed.

My dad continued talking about camp and his fears. About how his mother didn't teach him how to swim.

I thought it was strange that my father was telling a summer story during a Christmas Eve service. But I liked it. It worked somehow.

Then he started his usual ranting about the church.

He hated dogma. It stifled the spirit.

He wanted people to instead pay attention to their goosebumps and lumps in the throat. He said that was the Holy Spirit.

What about really random stoned thoughts? I wondered.

What about them? Is that the Holy Spirit?

What about loneliness?

What about boners?

I wanted to raise my hand and ask him about all that, but I figured it would be inappropriate. So I didn't. I figured I could ask him later. In private.

I slept soundly that night and in the morning we woke up and I gave Bella her presents.

I had gotten her a shit ton of cookbooks and some jewelry.

Jay didn't like opening presents. It made him anxious.

So I didn't get him anything. And I could tell he appreciated that.

Then we went to my father's.

We gave him his present and made him some food.

He talked to us while he ate. I hated when he talked with his mouth full.

But I held it in that day.

It was Christmas. The man deserved to act like a beast.

THE SWEET GLOW OF THE SCREEN

I took Jay to the movies. I figured it would be a good break from all the socializing I had been forcing him into.

My plan was for us to see three movies in a row. And he seemed excited about that.

The first movie we watched was *The Wolf Of Wall Street.*

I had no idea the movie was a comedy. It was like a million hours of rich guys partying too hard and it was hilarious.

We got out of the movie at three-ish.

Jay told me he was all movied out.

I was too.

So we went to my father's.

He was napping in bed.

We sat in the living room and waited for the bear to rise from the depths like an ancient elder god.

While we waited we turned on the TV.

We ended up watching a movie. A James L. Brooks movie. *I'll Do Anything*. A movie about fatherhood. Starring a very handsome Nick Nolte.

Jay got bored and escaped to my father's office and prowled the internet.

Bella came home around six.

We all ate.

I told Bella about *The Wolf Of Wall Street*.

She got mad at me. She got really mad.

"What the fuck, Grimby. You promised me that you would watch that movie with me. I'm so mad at you right now."

"I never promised you shit," I said.

"Here we go," Jay said.

"I'm just saying you promised me that you would see that movie with me, and you saw it without me and that's fucked up."

"This is what it's like being married," I said to Jay.

He didn't respond.

My father looked at us nervously.

We continued to battle.

"Why couldn't you just wait till I got home to watch that movie?" she asked.

"I don't know. We just didn't. Shit."

She started giving me the silent treatment.

My father turned a movie on.

Bella still looked really mad.

I tried to flirt with her.

It didn't work.

I even apologized.

It didn't work. She was still angry.

Finally I asked her to walk to my dad's office with me.

"Listen," I said. "You are overreacting and you need to stop. I was just trying to show our guest a good time."

"Jay's not a guest," she said. "He's family."

"He's also a guest. And I wanted to show him a good time. That's all. And you're being really awkward and making people uncomfortable. Have you noticed my dad hasn't even stood up for you? He's always on your side during an argument. He loves ganging up on me with you. But he hasn't. 'Cause you're being awkward. So stop."

We went back into the living room and continued watching the movie.

"You two okay?" my dad asked.

We didn't respond.

Eventually Bella apologized.

But I was too annoyed at this point.

So I just sat there, fuming.

She kept apologizing.

She tried to flirt with me.

I didn't respond.

HOUSEKEEPING

Jay wanted to pay us back for our hospitality by cleaning the house.

He wanted to start with Mount Dishberg. That's what we named the pile of dishes in the sink.

But we didn't have any sponges. We had washcloths.

Jay didn't like that.

"Can't handle," he kept saying. "Fucking washcloths. What is this, the 1800s?"

So we walked down to the Nelson's.

Nelson's is a shop in West Racine that sells all sorts of cheap stuff. Sponges. Winter hats. Army men. Diet Snapple. Yarn. Cap guns. Chocolate. Shoelaces. Gloves. Hats. Lawn gnomes. Stale popcorn. Green Bay Packers paraphernalia. Bumper stickers.

A whole bunch of years ago, when my grandfather got senile, he would go down to Nelson's a lot. He would walk in, grab a toy, then walk out without paying. Then he would send me the toy in the mail. Nelson's let him steal. They would call my father and he would pay for whatever it was Grandpa Grimbol had taken.

I told Jay about this.

He liked the story.

When I walked into the store, the lady behind the register saw me and laughed.

"Did you lose your hat again?" she asked.

Jay looked confused.

"I lose a lot of hats," I said.

"He's in here buying hats all the time," the lady said.

"Well, I didn't come here to buy a hat today. I came here to buy a sponge," I said.

"Really? Well, well, well. You know we got some new winter hats. Five bucks each."

I winced at her.

"Okay. Maybe I'll buy a hat too."

We bought the sponge then went home and did the dishes.

While we were cleaning, I started talking about all of our female friends that had babies.

So many of them had babies.

Jay looked sad.

I was surprised by how sullen this topic made him.

We were silent for a bit.

"I feel like the whole world has moved on and gotten married and I've been left behind. Everyone has these nice homes and I live in this tiny apartment. Alone."

I laughed. But it was a very sympathetic laugh. Or at least I hoped it was.

"You don't know how lucky you are," I said. "All this domesticity is exhausting. If I lived alone, I would be living in a one bedroom, with a futon on the ground, a desk, and a weight bench. I'd be walking around naked. And I would always have an erection. Always. 'Cause my soul would be just so turned on by how manly my life would be."

Jay shook his head.

"I don't know, man. You seem to enjoy the life you have. You still get to walk around your apartment naked. You get served breakfast in bed. Your woman is hilarious. And it's not like you would use the weight bench that much anyway."

"Hey, I work out."

"We haven't worked out much since I got here."

"That's 'cause it's the holidays."

"I'm just saying, you like your treats."

"Sure, but I also miss being single and living more simply."

"Your house isn't that cluttered."

"I guess not."

"The most cluttered room is your office."

"Good point."

"I just think that having someone, a partner or whatever,

would make life easier."

"In some ways it does," I said. "Sorta. Often it can make things harder. Like I like to move a lot. But Bella is just awful at it. She makes moving really hard on me. It's like *Legend of Zelda: Link to the Past.*"

"It's the best game ever," he said.

"Right. You remember the first level, you get your sword and you go to find the princess. The level is easy, until you find the princess, then you have to backtrack through the whole fucking level again. This time you're dragging her behind you, and it's much harder. You don't move as fast. You got her lagging behind getting stuck behind random shit. When she gets hit by a bad guy, you lose heart points. She makes you more vulnerable."

"It's a good metaphor or analogy or whatever."

"Thanks."

"But Bella is stronger than you in a lot of ways. I mean, she's real responsible and shit. The girl loves to cook and keep track of your banking."

I laughed.

"You're saying I'm the princess."

"No, I'm just saying. Sure, she sucks at moving. But she's better at bills and cooking."

"And she's better at being happy."

"She's really happy," he said. "Fucking girl is happy as hell."

"Very."

"But she sucks at moving. I'm sure that's hard."

"It sucks. I love to move. Just talking about it gets her nervous."

"I hate moving too," he said.

He finished the dishes and we went to the living room and watched the snow fall.

"Fuck, it's like a fucking scene from *Frankenstein*," he said.

I didn't get that.

"What do you mean?" I said.

"You know when he finds the monster in the North Pole."

"Isn't that the pole where Santa Claus lives?"

"I think so. Didn't Tim Allen play Santa Claus once?"

"I think he played him a few times."

"Ugh, that's disgusting," Jay said. "I hate Tim Allen."

"Me too, me too. Just seeing him fills me with rage."

"What was that show he had? *Tool Time*. Or was it *Home Improvement*?"

"It was awful. It was the worst thing ever created," I said.

"The kids on *Home Improvement* were so annoying," he said,

"They looked like date rapists," I said.

"I know," he said. "They really did."

He looked back outside.

"I get nervous sometimes," I said.

"What do you mean?"

"Sometimes when the weather gets really nasty I think the world might be ending."

"Like that movie *The Day After Tomorrow*?"
I nodded.
"Exactly like that movie."
"I actually like that movie," he said.
"Me too."

THE WORLD ENDS.
PUPPIES TAKE OVER.
HEARTS EXPLODE.

It was New Year's Eve.

Jay said he wanted to get drunk.

"Don't say that," I begged. "Every time you start talking about how hard you want to party, you end up not partying. And then whenever you don't want to party you end up getting drunk as hell."

"Do I really do that?"

"Every time. It's like a scientific fact by now."

"Why do you think I do that?" he asked.

"It's like you put too much pressure on yourself and then you get anxiety," I said.

"Probably true."

"It happens every time."

He walked to the kitchen and grabbed a beer.

"Maybe this time I'll surprise you."

I smiled at him. My smile was filled with teeth and love.

He saw this and embraced me.

He had strong arms.

"Where are we partying tonight?" he asked.

"My buddy Ron's house," I said.

We sat around and drank beer and talked about parties of the past.

Thick flakes of snow fell from the sky.

Bella got home from work at eight and she looked like she had just gotten off a roller coaster.

"That was intense," she said. "I saw like four cars stuck on the side of the road on my way back from work."

I gave her a hug.

"Let's go party," I said.

"I need to shower first."

Jay and I had some more drinks and waited.

Once Bella was ready we got in the Jeep and headed out.

We drove slowly.

The snow had piled up high and the roads didn't look like roads at all and I felt excited. I felt adventurous.

I walked into Ron's house and noticed everyone taking off their shoes and leaving them at the door. My boots were wet and I didn't want to leave little puddles around his place, but my socks were crusty and stank.

Bella noticed me drying my boots with a napkin. She knew what I was doing.

"Don't do that," she said. "Just take your boots off. Nobody will notice your stinky socks."

"You sure?"

She smiled.

"I'm sorta sure," she said.

My buddy Ron introduced me to his new puppy.

"Happy New Year," he said. "This is Max."

I told him his puppy was cute and introduced him to Jay.

"Look at that little thing," Jay said.

He petted the dog and let it nibble on his hand a little.

We grabbed a beer and gathered in the living room with the rest of the guests.

Bella loved the puppy.

She wanted a dog. I didn't.

I liked to move around and a dog would make that difficult. It would make many things difficult.

Most of the conversations that night involved the puppy and how to train it. I found it hard to watch and I knew Jay was having a hard time with it as well.

"Where did you get that thing?" he asked.

"Pet Land," Ron said.

"Pet Land? I heard they put little bombs in their puppies' hearts so you have to buy a new one in a couple years."

I laughed. Nobody else laughed though.

They ignored the morbid comment and continued discussing the dog and how to keep it from nibbling on everyone.

Eventually they put the dog in its cage and the party got a bit livelier.

I got drunk and started dancing with all the women. I didn't grind up on any butts like I usually would. I felt too goofy. Instead I just pranced and shook my own butt at everyone and made jokes.

At midnight everyone hooted and cheered and took shots to celebrate the New Year.

Bella kissed me. Her lips were very warm.

"I want a puppy," she said.

"I'll give you some of my puppy," I said.

I grabbed her, held her close, and humped her a little.

She laughed.

I heard my friend Paul and his wife smooching.

He was telling her all the raunchy things he wanted to do to her. I overheard all this and got excited.

"Woooeee! That's some kinky stuff."

I gave them a big hug.

People saw us all hugging and joined in. It turned into a big group hug.

Jay didn't join in. He was in the living room sulking.

I stumbled over to him and we talked.

"I feel like the whole world has gotten married," he said.

I told him he should join one of those dating sites.

"That's what I would do if I was single," I said. "They seem like fun."

He said he would try it out. But I knew that wasn't true. He didn't like the internet. He was too reclusive for that sort of thing.

We started talking about his paintings.

His paintings were very simple. Usually they were portraits of friends looking like they were from some unrecognizable bygone era. He loved all those old religious paintings. And it showed in his work.

But that night he said he wanted to paint a Robocop. It was his favorite movie. Whenever he got uncomfortable he talked about *Robocop*.

I looked over and saw Katy dancing. She was wearing tight black pants and her ass was shaking so much I could barely stand it. I was having one of those spiritual moments. It was like some crazy god light was shooting out of her butt crack.

"SHAKE IT GIRL!" I yelled.

"Yeah!" Jay yelled.

Katy turned around, looking embarrassed.

She walked up and hit me.

"What the fuck?"

"That's to remind you that we are just friends," she said.

"Shit, I know that. But that doesn't mean I'm not a man with the needs of a man and sometimes when I see a butt shake like that I feel like I gotta say something about it."

Jay smiled. "So true," he said. "What can I say, the man's a poet."

She walked off and Jay and I kept talking about *Robocop* and painting and painting Robocop and how to make that image spiritual somehow.

We drank more and joked around.

Around two, people got tired.

Katy had her dog with her. He was a massive thing.

"How long is your dog supposed to live for?" Jay asked her.

She got really sad looking and walked away.

Jay was confused.

"Was that an offensive thing to ask?"

"I don't know," I said.

We were all drunk so we slept in Ron's living room that night.

He put the movie *Hot Tub Time Machine* on for us.

I passed out within ten minutes and woke up to the menu screen playing over and over again.

I turned the TV off.

"Good job, Eddie," Jay said.

He was lying on the floor.

I laughed.

Bella laughed too.

I was shocked. Usually she was impossible to wake.

We lay around for a bit, trying to fall back to sleep, but I was too uncomfortable.

"I'm so stiff," Jay said.

"I feel like I have Parkinson's," I said.

Bella and Jay laughed.

"Let's get the fuck out of here," I said.

We got up and searched for our shoes and our jackets.

The dog woke up and started barking.

I told it to shut up.

It yelped and clawed at its cage.

I drove home slowly because I was still a little drunk and the roads were covered in snow.

We got home and sat in the living room for a bit.

The sun was rising. It was morning.

Our apartment was thrashed.

"I like your apartment," Jay said. "Your friend's apartment was too fancy. Your apartment is cozy."

We chatted for a bit longer, then we went to bed.

We slept until noon.

IDIOT'S GUIDE TO EATING FOOD

We didn't have any measuring cups. Bella usually just guessed the amount of crap she put in stuff.

Jay didn't like that. It made him anxious. Very anxious.

He wanted to make pancakes.

He had been talking about pancakes the whole visit.

"I give up," he said. "I need a measuring cup."

Bella helped him out and made the mix the right consistency.

He started to calm down. Then he noticed we didn't have the right kind of oil.

"Can't make pancakes without the right oil," he kept saying.

"It's fine," Bella said. "It just needs a teaspoon. It won't affect the flavor. It just helps it rise. Relax."

I laughed.

HARD BODIES

Jay's eyes were wide and filled with panic.

I suggested eating out.

Bella got upset and started whining.

I decided to go outside and shovel some snow and ignore the situation.

The sidewalk was covered in a thick layer of snow.

I shoveled fast. Got out of breath.

Cursed the snow for being so obnoxious and dumb.

Then I went back inside and took a shower.

The warm water felt good.

Real good.

I LIKE IT RAW

Bella made us huge omelets stuffed with cheese and veggies.

We sat at our dining room table.

It was a small round table.

We ate.

"Too much cheese," Jay told us.

And he picked at his food.

He explained why he didn't like too much cheese on things.

That night we decided to make a meal for my dad.

Jay insisted we make the old man chicken cordon bleu.

We liked that idea.

He said he wanted to find a recipe online.

Bella told him that wasn't necessary.

"I just think it's good to have a recipe," he said.

"But I have made this so many times," Bella said.

"I like using the recipe."

"Jay," I said. "Chicken cordon bleu sounds fancy, but it's simple. Using a recipe is silly. It would be like needing a recipe to make a grilled cheese sandwich."

We drove to the grocery store and got the ingredients.

Then we drove to my dad's.

Bella made the meal and it looked perfect.

I brought my dad his plate first.

He was sitting in his La-Z-Boy. He used his big belly as a table.

Then I got my own plate.

I tore into the chicken. It looked too shiny. Too moist. I realized it wasn't fully cooked.

We all brought our plates back to the kitchen, so Bella could continue baking the meat in the oven.

My dad kept eating.

We yelled "stop!"

There was a mad dash.

We had to save my father from eating too much raw chicken.

Jay got to his plate first. He grabbed it.

My dad held tight.

He continued eating.

I grabbed the plate and finally ripped it from his sweaty hands.

He looked confused.

We explained why you don't eat raw chicken.

"It tasted fine though," he kept saying.

Bella re-cooked the chicken and then brought it back out. The chicken looked mangled but tasty.

But Jay wouldn't eat it now. He felt too paranoid.

He ate the rice and the salad and all the veggies, but he had decided he didn't like meat anymore.

While we ate he told us he wanted to be a vegetarian.

My dad and Bella and I spent the rest of the night watching *Downton Abbey*.

Jay hid in my dad's office, looking up old paintings on the internet.

Hours passed.

Jay came out to join us.

In one of the scenes an aristocratic old lady explains to a rich young man that gentlemen don't work.

I liked that notion.

"I guess that means I'm a gentleman," I said.

The next day Jay left.

I had given him a bunch of books to read.

When we got to the train station we hugged.

Then I drove to my dad's.

I sat on his couch and watched TV. Too much TV.

Then I got back in my Jeep.

I saw the stack of books I gave Jay in the back.

Jay was always avoiding the books I wanted him to read.

I decided to mail him the books.

I was going to text Jay and guilt-trip him.

But I decided against it.

I drove home.

I masturbated.

I showered.

I ate food.

Bella came home from work.

She was grumpy.

She caught a staff member bullying a kid.

That happened a lot.

People in her field are not as kind hearted as they should be.

Bella talked to the lady who was mean to the kid.

The woman got really hurt and acted as wounded as possible.

Bella felt guilty and confused.

I held her and told her she did a good job.

Then she told me about another kid who was paralyzed.

Some men that worked there had restrained him improperly.

They broke his back.

Now he couldn't walk.

"I want to watch so many hours of *Downton Abbey* tonight," she said. "Then I want to watch *The Mindy Project*, then I want to watch more TV. Endless TV."

I laughed.
She got up.
Walked to the kitchen.
Noticed the sink was filled with dishes.
We fought about the dishes for a while.

GLOW IN THE DARK VACATIONS
AND
OTHER NIGHTMARE VISIONS OF THE
FUTURE

The soundtrack to *Downton Abbey* was very eerie, but in a sentimental way. And it made me feel out of it and sweet.

I loved the show. Living in that big ass house/castle thing with all those people seemed like fun. I imagined it was like camp.

"This show's amazing," I said to my father.

He was sitting in his La-Z-Boy wearing one of his shorter nightgowns.

I could see his balls. They were huge.

"Get me a Diet Coke," he said.

"Dad, I'm trying to have an emotional moment with you. I'm trying to bond over the emotional impact this show has had on our lives."

"Get me a Diet Coke first," he said.

He was using his baby voice. I hated that baby voice.

I walked to the kitchen. I poured him a glass of Diet Coke and got myself a couple of clementines.

My father saw the clementines and got annoyed.

"Hey, I want clementines too," he said.

The old man had trouble seeing food. As soon as he saw something he wanted to eat it. I was afraid that one day his hunger would get worse and that he would start eating everything he saw. Couches. Cars. People.

I passed him one of my clementines.

He looked frustrated. I hadn't peeled it for him.

I sat and we finished watching our show.

Bella got bored of the couch she was lying on, so she rolled onto the ground.

My dad looked at her and laughed.

"You know what I want to buy you guys for your anniversary next year?" he said.

"What?" I asked.

"A trip to the Caribbean."

Bella's eyes lit up.

"That will be so much fun!" she said.

I was annoyed.

"Fuck, don't do this to me!" I said.

"What's your problem?" my dad asked.

"I don't want to go to the fucking Caribbean and hang out

in some tacky ass tourist thingy with a bunch of people that look like they belong in the audience of the Oprah show. Fuck."

"Where would you want to go?" my father asked.

I wanted to go to some magical land where everyone was sloppy and the women smelled like stinky armpits. Like the hippy girls I met in high school. I mean girls with full beards under their arms. Big messy armpits. Rowdy armpits. I wanted to go to a place that was lonely and haunted and covered in dense pine forests and big mountains and old men that partied with young people and gave them bad advice. That's what I wanted. That was my Narnia. Fucking place. Fucking place only sort of existed.

"Shit," I said. "I don't know. Maybe like the Canadian Rockies or…"

"NO!" Bella yelled.

She rolled on her back and kicked her legs in the air.

"I want to go somewhere warm," she said.

She did love the sun. There was no denying that. Her hair got blonder. Her laughter got fuller. Her skirts got weirder and more colorful and looser.

I couldn't deny her the sun.

It had been a harsh winter. It snowed nonstop.

And the Weather Channel said it was only going to get worse.

Rumor had it they were closing schools on Monday because it was supposed to be negative sixteen degrees with a wind chill of negative fifty.

No, I couldn't deny Bella the sun.

"I got a compromise," I said. "How 'bout Florida."

"We can go to the Keys," she said.

"Sure, we'll make a road trip out of it. We'll see lots of shit. We can even go to Georgia and see that town *Fried Green Tomatoes* was filmed in."

She rolled her eyes.

"Everything has to be a road trip with you," she said.

We started fighting.

I didn't want to be a tacky tourist.

She didn't want to be a tacky overly bohemian fuck up.

My dad lost interest in the conversation.

His initial gift had been ignored. It had mutated into something strange to him.

He looked at me.

I looked at him.

I could see his huge balls.

"I want a diet soda," he said.

BELLA UNLEASHED

"BELLA!" I yelled.

I was in bed. Naked. So, so naked.

"BELLA!" I kept yelling.

I reached for the door. Opened it.

"BELLA! DEAR GOD! I NEED ATTENTION! PLEASE! COME HERE!"

I could hear her. I could hear her doing things.

I kept calling for her.

Finally, she came to my room.

"Hey honey."

"Let's have sex," I said.

"I gotta go."

"NO!" I yelled.

I reached for her crotch.

She dodged me. She dodged my chubby little hands and

my little fingers.

"I got to go to the gym and then to work," she said. "I don't have time to do stuff with your stinky little body."

"DEAR LORD I'M BEGGING YOU! HAVE MERCY!"

She laughed and dodged my chubby grasp again.

I wanted her. I wanted to smell her vagina and hump her and say really tacky raunchy things to her and to come and then to go back to sleep.

"You do this every Thursday," she said. "Every Thursday, you wait until I'm about to leave and then you try to have sex with me."

"I do?"

"Why don't you just wait until I get home?"

"You want me to wait ten hours?"

I took the blankets off my body. I showed her my cock. It was hard.

"Look at this thing."

"It is really cute."

"It's a monster."

She walked away.

"Can you just touch it a little?"

"No," she said.

I looked out the window. Our back yard was covered in snow.

I looked on the floor. My pocket pussy was hiding next to a stack of books.

No, that wouldn't be enough. I was feeling emotionally

needy.

I got up and stumbled through the house naked.

Bella saw me and gave me a hug.

I humped her a little.

"Stop," she said.

I pretended to cry. She thought that was funny.

"Can you remember to pay the water bill today, and to take out the trash, and to do the dishes? And remember, you need to go to the gym."

"I hate your lists," I said. "You're such a task master blaster."

"Am not. Could you also go to the grocery store and get more milk?"

"Dear GOD YOU ARE RELENTLESS!"

"Stop being so dramatic."

"You know I don't like it when you plan my day like this."

"I'm not planning your day. I just need help doing a few things."

"That was way more than a few things."

She kissed me on the cheek.

Then she walked out the door.

I heard the car start then pull away.

I thought about all the things she wanted me to do. It made me feel old.

I'm a grownup, I kept thinking. I got stuff to do.

My phone beeped.

I walked into my room and dug my phone out of my laundry pile.

There was a text from Bella.

Remember to go to the gym today, it said.

Then she texted me a smiley face.

I threw the phone back into the dirty laundry pile and I shook my fists in the air and yelled, "NEVER!"

WEED

We sat on either end of the couch. Bella was covered in blankets.

She only let me have a little bit of the blankets. Just enough to cover my feet. Which was important. My feet were really cold.

"I miss weed," she said.

"Me too."

"Wisconsin hates weed. My job hates weed. Stupid piss tests."

"How long has it been?" I asked.

"Almost a year," she said.

"It feels like a zillion years."

"More like a billion."

"Ummm, a zillion is more than a billion."

"Is not."

"Is too," I said, standing my ground.

Bella sighed.

It was the first time she had ever had a job that did random piss tests. She was dealing with it well, but every once in a while she got real homesick for it.

"I bet if I smoked I could get away with it," she said.

"Probably. They piss tested us at that rehab I worked at. I would smoke with you every once in a while and it would be really fun, but then I would get all paranoid for the rest of the week."

"I don't like being paranoid."

"Nobody likes being paranoid."

"But you have anxiety issues. Maybe I wouldn't get paranoid."

"Trust me, you would get paranoid," I said.

She smiled.

I knew what she was thinking. She was remembering one of my many anxiety attacks and thinking about how hilarious it was.

"Remember that time we were driving to Texas and you took like two hits of weed and started freaking out?" she asked.

"I took way more than two hits. And yes. I felt like I was driving at some impossibly fast speed. Like I was going warp nine."

"Is that a *Star Trek* reference?" she asked.

"Yes. Yes it is."

She made an angry face.

Bella didn't like *Star Trek*. She didn't like anything dorky and she was very verbal about it.

"You liked the last *Star Trek* movie," I said.

"Not really."

She looked out the window. It was snowing. It had been snowing on and off for over a week.

"Remember that one winter we lived with your dad on Shelter Island?" she said.

I nodded.

"Remember smoking weed and walking around the grave-yard?"

"It was a good time," I said. "Except my aunt was visiting and she was sleeping on the couch and if you tried to leave the house at night she would wake up and freak out and have one of her hissy fits."

"Then how did we manage to go for that walk and smoke in the graveyard?"

"We ended up waking her up. We got into tons of shit about it in the morning. It was a big deal."

"Was it?"

"Yeah, remember? I got into that crazed argument with her. I told her it was normal to go for walks at night. She was concerned that we were going to get mugged."

Bella laughed.

We were silent for bit.

A snow plow drove down our street and I enjoyed hearing

it scraping its shovel against the road.

"You wanna have sex?" I asked.

"Sure, why not."

We walked into our room.

She got on the bed.

I took off my pants.

"Oh man, you need to take a shower."

I thought about it. Being all soapy and warm seemed nice.

"Okay," I said. "But you wait right here."

"I'll join you," she said.

"Don't. I like it when you're stinky."

"But one time you said I smelled like a urinal."

"That time you were a little too stinky."

"Still, it was a really mean thing to say. And what if I'm too stinky right now?"

"Stop trying to start a fight," I said.

I went to the bathroom and turned the shower on.

I looked at my naked chest in the mirror.

I flexed my muscles and made an angry face.

My man boobs looked awesome. Why was I so embarrassed by them? I wondered.

I put my hand under the stream of water to check the temperature. It was hot enough.

I got in the shower and washed my body. I moved quickly because I had a boner and wanted to do sex stuff.

When I got back to my room Bella was under the blankets. She looked cozy.

"You ready for the hurricane? The hurricane of dick!"

She reached out and grabbed it.

"You go to the gym today?" she asked.

"Can you not nag me about going to the gym?" I said. "We are about to bone out."

"Sorry."

"Jesus. Nagging me about the gym is so unsexy."

She got on all fours.

Her butthole put me in a trance.

I leaned over and smelled it. It had a smoky tangy meaty aroma.

I moaned.

I licked the butthole.

I put my dick in her ass cheeks.

My phone started ringing. The sound was faint. It was hiding somewhere in the room.

I ignored it.

Bella moaned.

I put my dick in. Her pussy was wet and easy to fit into.

We did all the basic stuff, but with a bit more enthusiasm than normal.

After we had both gotten off, we snuggled in bed.

"I miss weed," she said.

"I know."

"Maybe I should treat it like more of a priority and get a job that doesn't do drug tests."

"I wouldn't worry about it," I said. "You should treat your

job as a priority. It's a good job."

My phone started ringing again.

I got up and looked for it.

It was buried deep in the dirty laundry pile gathered in the corner of the room.

It said I had five missed calls.

The most recent was from my aunt Jacky.

Bella's phone rang.

"It's Jacky," she said.

"You going to answer it?"

She shook her head.

"That is one intense old lady," Bella said.

"She's terrifying," I said.

Bella smiled.

"She's not that bad."

"She's basically a Ringwraith," I said.

"Is that a weird nerdy *Star Trek* reference?"

"*Lord of the Rings*," I said.

"Dear God, you're not into that now?"

"No, I hate *Lord of The Rings*."

"Then why do you keep referencing it?"

"I only referenced it once. Calm down."

"You calm down."

"I want a Gatorade," I said.

"You can't, you're on a diet."

"I know."

I looked out the window.

"It stopped snowing," I said.

"Finally," Bella said.

"Nope, wait, it started again."

"This is the worst winter ever," she said.

She looked at her phone.

"Real feel is negative three."

"I wish I could remember what the real feel was when we lived in Vermont."

"They didn't use that term back then," she said.

"I know. But I don't even remember knowing what the wind chill was back then."

"I don't think it was as bad as this."

"I do."

"No, it wasn't."

"I think it was worse at times."

"I miss Vermont," she said. "I miss weed."

"Me too. But I like it here too."

"Me too."

"What should we do now?" I asked.

"Don't know."

"Let's go to my dad's and watch TV."

"I guess. But are we boring for wanting to go to your dad's to hang out all the time?"

"I wouldn't worry about it."

We got dressed and I packed my computer into my backpack so I could use my father's internet.

The snow intensified. We drove slowly.

Bella noticed I wasn't nervous.

"You're doing so good, honey," she said. "You're, like, not totally terrified of the snow."

"I got my driving mojo back, baby. My PTSD from that horrible accident is almost completely gone. Sorta. I've been driving in the snow every fucking day and now I'm totally fucking used to it. I'm a fucking demon on the road. Watch out Mother Earth, I'm going to leave skid marks on your stomach."

"Skid marks? Like poop stains?"

"I meant to say tire marks," I said.

"Oh, I get it," she said. "That's funny."

GROCERY STORE XXX

The parking lot in front of the Pick N Save was packed.

"It's busy," Bella said as she pulled into a parking space. "I'm surprised it's so busy."

"You say that every time we go shopping," I said.

"I do?"

"You do."

We got out and wobbled into the store.

There was so much food. But no smell.

I walked alongside my wife, in a trance.

There was a woman with long braids and tight zebra striped leggings and a huge butt. She was in the dairy section and she made me feel magical, like if I unzipped my pants a mighty eagle would fly out and bury its talons in her ass cheeks.

Bella caught me staring.

"That's so much butt," she said.

"I know. All I want is to sniff it, just once. Just once."

She laughed.

"What if it smells bad?" she asked.

"I just want to snuggle with it," I said.

Bella rolled her eyes.

I got bored of shopping and snuck off to the magazine rack.

There were a couple of rap magazines and the rap magazines had pictures of big butted ladies and I liked to look at those pictures and imagine what the butts felt like and smelled like and this made my heart go pitter patter and it made my soul glow in the dark and it made ghosts of butts past come down from the heavens and party in my wiener, like my wiener was just a tower people liked to party in.

There were also romance novels. I thought about buying one of these romance novels. And reading it.

But then I decided that would be boring and horrible so I didn't do that.

I started thinking about butts again. I thought about all the butts of the world and how terrifying they must smell. I wanted to smell them all. I wanted to take a weekend off from all my typing and reading and family stuff and just smell butts.

Bella made a big veggie pie that night.

It tasted good. But not as good as it usually tasted.

Usually we got our veggies from a farm stand outside of town.

HARD BODIES

It was run by this old couple. They would sit there covered in flies, looking sleepy and content.

We would order our veggies.

They would take their time adding up our total.

The old lady wanted to make sure we were on her mailing list. She wanted to send us a Christmas card.

We must have given that old biddy our address a dozen times. But we didn't get a card in the mail.

Maybe they're dead.

Hope not.

WHAT IT'S LIKE TO MAKE LOVE TO SOMEONE YOU LOVE A WHOLE BUNCH AND WHO MAKES YOU FOOD AND HAS A BIG BUTT AND BIG EYES AND STUFF

My wifey and I woke up feeling groggy and soft.

She made us eggs.

We ate in bed, then cuddled.

We cuddled and kissed each other. I licked her belly and her nipples.

I put my fingers into her vagina until it was extra gooey.

I licked the vagina too.

"Less rough," she said.

"Rough?"

"Yeah, like, you know, less rough."

"Right."

I eased up and worked the clit like it was a little dick. Like it was a little Micro Machine dick. Like it was a dick that was shrunken by a giant laser whose sole purpose was to shrink things. Like it was a little bunny dick.

Anyway, I licked her clitty.

My dick got hard.

I took my sweatpants off. For some reason I had slept in my sweatpants, which is strange for me, cause I usually sleep in the nude.

I put my dick in the gooey vagina.

I humped her.

And as I humped, I kept my face close to hers and I kissed her and tried to put my tongue in her mouth, so it could snuggle with her tongue, but she wouldn't let me in.

"It's too early in the morning," she said. "Your breath smells weird."

I went down on her again and put it in her again.

She got on all fours and I did her that way.

She rubbed her clit as I humped.

She moaned and her pussy got all tight.

She made her angry face and then she came.

Then she tried to finish me off orally.

I wanted it deep in her mouth but she ended up gagging. And not in a sexy way.

"Still too early in the morning. I got eggs in my mouth from breakfast."

I didn't like that. Why did she have to mention breakfast like that? I was trying to feel sexy.

But I put it behind me because I figured she had the post-orgasm grumpies.

And who wanted dick stirring up all sorts of eggs and cheese and potatoes and other breakfast crap?

It's important to be a sympathetic lover so I stopped aiming my dick at her face and climbed on top of her.

"I love you," I said.

"I love you too," she said.

"Please don't talk about breakfast while we're having sex?" I said.

"Sorrrrry," she said, sounding annoyed. "But your dick made me want to puke up my omelet right then."

Okay. That did it. I wasn't in the mood any longer and I told her so.

"No, keep going," she said.

"No, I don't find your bratty bullshit sexy."

I got off and turned my back to her.

"Why are you overreacting?" she said.

"'Cause you have been acting like a brat all Christmas break and I am at my wit's end. I don't like having boners when you are being Christmas bratcicle."

We lay there in silence for a while.

I started reading my Kindle.

She started reading her book as well. Her book was made out of paper, not electricity, like mine.

Eventually we stopped reading and looked at each other.

"How are you feeling?" I asked.

"I feel bad. I feel bad 'cause I acted like a brat and I feel bad 'cause you scolded me."

"I feel bad 'cause you keep ruining shit."

"What do you mean? I don't ruin things!"

"Like last night. It was so cozy. We ate great food."

"Which I made," she said.

"Right, fine, sure. And it was super nice. My dad and I got along, which is rare, and we watched like a million hours of *Downton Abbey* and everything felt all good and shit and then you went and got all crabby from being tired and you started acting bitchy and ruined that good feeling."

"I was tired. I didn't want to be at your dad's anymore."

There was more silence.

Then she said, "Well, maybe I'm just feeling irritable 'cause you don't work and you have so much free time and I don't."

"Fuck off!" I yelled. "You know I try to make your days off awesome. I do whatever I can to make your days off the best days off in the whole wide world. You're the one that ruins shit by getting all bratty. THIS MORNING COULD HAVE BEEN BLISSFUL! IT COULD HAVE BEEN FUCKING HEAVENLY! IT COULD HAVE BEEN MOTHERFUCKING HEAVEN ON EARTH!"

"So this is my fault? All of it. You can't take any of the blame?"

"Jesus, I hate that argument tactic. You and my dad always do that. It's such a cop out. Instead of just seeing the argument through, you turn it into an argument about how we argue.”

"I just think you might be overreacting just a little bit.”

“Maybe I like overreacting.”

“Maybe I don't. 'Cause I work all the time and go to the gym and shit.”

We lay there. Staring off.

It was the third round of giving each other the silent treatment and I was getting tired.

I apologized for being mean.

She apologized for being bratty.

Neither of us were really that sorry. But it didn't matter.

I started flirting with her again. I made her giggle.

“You wanna finish me off?” I asked.

“Sure.”

“You wanna finish me off with the pocket pussy?”

“I don't get it. Pocket pussy? What's that slang for?”

I laughed.

“It's not slang for anything,” I said. “I want you to use that pocket pussy you got me for Christmas.”

“Really?”

I nodded.

She went into our closet. But the pocket pussy wasn't in there.

She went to the bathroom. I heard her laugh.

“I love how you keep the pocket pussy on the sink, next to our tooth brushes.”

I liked her laugh. It came from a deep and goofy and

clumsy part of her soul.

She walked into the room.

I took the blanket off and showed her my medium sized penis.

She put lube on it.

Then she put the pocket pussy on it.

She moved it up and down.

I moaned and started acting all sexy.

"I'm going to come," I said.

She moved the pocket pussy down so my dick head came out the other end of it.

I squirted semen out of my dick hole and it shot all the way to my armpit.

"Wow!" she said. "That was awesome."

She rolled onto her back and laughed a deeply clumsy laugh.

I got up.

I smiled.

I wasn't tired.

Usually coming makes me tired.

But I wasn't tired. I was awake.

I was fully awake.

I got out of bed and started dancing like I was a ballerina. I knew this would make my giant flubby body look hilarious.

Bella liked what I was doing. It made her laugh.

MARY'S

Our apartment looked clean. Too clean.

Bella was on the couch surrounded by paperwork.

She was talking to someone on the phone and her voice sounded super responsible.

When she got off the phone she looked up at me and smiled but it didn't seem to be a very sincere smile, but that might just be from my intense mistrust of all things responsible and clean.

"Honey," she said. "Do you want me to set you up a dentist appointment for the same day as mine?"

I got angry.

"Damn it, Bella, I told you I don't want to go to the dentist. I've told you that so many times. Can you please fuck off? Stop trying to control me!"

I stomped off into my room.

I sat at the edge of my bed and stared out the window.

It was a surprisingly warm day. It was almost forty degrees. I wanted to be outside, prancing around.

Bella came in.

She didn't like that I yelled at her.

We started fighting.

She thought I was being neurotic and unreasonable. I thought she was being pushy.

Eventually she stormed off.

I decided to get some fresh air and buy some laces for my boots at Nelson's.

Everything outside looked wet. The snow was melting. There were puddles everywhere.

I saw this one kid. He was shoveling water. It seemed like a very lonely thing to do.

I waved at him.

He waved back.

The women that work at Nelson's are usually very nice to me. Not that day.

It was like they could tell I had just yelled at my woman. And they were mad at me about it.

"Do you have any shoe laces?" I asked this one lady.

"Of course we do. Aisle three. Toward the back."

I got back home and laced up my boots.

Bella was in the kitchen cooking.

She was still giving me the silent treatment.

Or maybe I was giving her the silent treatment. It was hard to tell.

Hours passed.

Eventually both of us went into the living room. I sat in my favorite chair. She sat on the couch and we stared at each other.

Things were tense.

"Sorry I got too pushy," she said.

"Sorry I'm neurotic and unhealthy on an emotional level sometimes."

"It's okay."

"You want to go to Milwaukee and get Vietnamese food?"

She got really excited. She got up and started hopping around.

"I love Vietnamese food!" she yelled.

She did a few jump kicks.

I watched her and felt happy.

We drove to Milwaukee as the sun was setting. By the time we got there it was dark.

The restaurant was closed.

"There has to be another Vietnamese food place in Milwaukee. Or at least some Thai. Let's just drive around."

"I want Vietnamese food so bad!" she said.

She looked possessed.

I smiled at her nervously.

We journeyed onward.

While we were driving into the city I saw a restaurant called Mary's Burgers.

"Hey, I've heard of that place. I think it's run by drag queens," I said.

"That's neat."

"Neat. That's the coolest thing I've ever heard. Let's go."

"I was kinda looking forward to Vietnamese food."

I started pouting. My pouting could get real intense. It wasn't easy to be around.

"What's wrong?" Bella asked.

"I just think we should go to Mary's. It would be an adventure."

She pulled the car over.

Now she was pouting too.

Two Grimbolis pouting could be deadly.

"I'm just so bored," I said. "I need some adventure."

"Drag queens are an adventure?"

"Sort of. I mean, it's different at least. We've never been to a place like this before. We get Asian food all the time."

"We haven't had good Vietnamese food in months."

"I mean in the long run. How many times have you gone to some Vietnamese food place?"

"Lots of times."

"How many times have you been to a burger joint run by drag queens?"

"Never. But I really wanted tea."

"That's literally the most boring thing you have ever said."
She sighed.

"I guess you're right. Let's go."

We drove back to Mary's and walked in.

The place was covered in memorabilia crap. Our table was Betty Boop-themed. There was a huge poster of Madonna on the wall. It was from her appearance in *Dick Tracy*.

"Have you ever seen *Dick Tracy*?" I asked.

"You know how much I hate nerdy things," Bella said.

"Madonna was so damn sexy in that movie. So soft. So, so soft."

Our waiter came over. He looked like a normal old man. He even had a crew cut.

But then he started talking. This guy was sassy. He had pizazz. He had razzmatazz. It wasn't on full force that night. But it was there. I could sense it.

We ordered some coffee.

And, as he walked off, I noticed he walked more gracefully than most old men. And besides, how many old men with crew cuts work as waiters?

"I think he's a drag queen," I said.

"You do?"

I nodded.

"That's cool, I guess."

She smiled and looked at her menu.

"I guess I'll just get a cheeseburger," she said.

"C'mon, get the BJ burger. I don't know why they call it

that, but it has tons of guacamole in it.”

“No, I just want a NORMAL cheeseburger.”

“Jesus, you are boring tonight.”

“Am not.”

“Are too.”

“Am not.”

“Are too.”

“Am . . . not . . .”

“You are impossible to please,” I said.

“What’s your problem?” she said.

“How can you not be getting into this place?”

“Maybe I just don’t like you yelling at me all the time.”

I took her hand.

“I’m sorry,” I said. “I just want things to be exciting and fun.”

She smiled and it was a very warm smile.

“This place is kinda cool. The music they’re playing is nuts.”

They were playing Marky Mark and the Funky Bunch.

“Drag queens must really like the ’90s,” Bella said.

“I think they do.”

The waiter came back and we ordered our food.

While we waited for our food we talked about the book I was working on.

“Are there going to be awkward sex scenes with me in it?” she asked.

“So many,” I said. “But don’t worry, I’ll change your

name. Nobody will know it's you."

We started working on a list of names.

"Stella, that's a good name," I said. "Or Madonna. Or maybe Jasmine. Or . . ."

"Those are all drag queen names," she said.

"Whoops. I guess you're right."

We continued thinking about names until our food came, then we gorged ourselves.

The burgers were delicious.

And I felt good.

My belly was full.

I drank like nine cups of coffee.

Soon I was dancing in my seat. Bella watched me and laughed.

"I like it here," I said. "This is my kinda place."

Bella shook her head.

"Baby. Having big man boobs doesn't make you a drag queen," she said.

I smiled.

Then I grabbed one of my man boobs and shook it at her.

I winked at her.

I was acting sexy.

"Face it," I said. "I'm sexy in all sorts of ways."

"You are adorable."

"No, sexy."

"Same thing."

"Not the same thing."

TRANS MORPHERS
TRANSFAT
TRANSPORTATION (?)

Bella came into my office. I was working on a poem.

The poem was about butts.

I wanted to write a whole book about butts. Call it *Frankenbooty*.

"What the fuck is that?" Bella asked.

"It's *Frankenbooty*. It's going to be the next great American novel. Or poem. Or whatever."

"No. I mean that pile of trash in the corner of your room."

I looked over. An impressive pile of old photos, DVD cases, shitty books and other junk had gathered in the corner of the room.

"Are you building a nest?" she asked.

"No way. Just a pile. You know how I like piles."

"You sure do."

"I was thinking about putting a blanket over it."

"That's not a bad idea."

"You don't want me to clean it?"

"I mean, I do. I do want you to clean it. But that's a really intense pile. I wouldn't even know where to begin."

She was wearing fuzzy red sweat pants she got from my stepmom. They were baggy and cozy looking.

I grabbed her pants and pulled her close. I smelled her crotch.

She laughed and told me to stop.

"I can't help it. I have a libido. It fills me with passion."

"Oh baby," she said.

And she started trying to get it on by kissing my neck and grabbing my dick.

"Stop," I said. "I can't do that right now. I gotta write."

"Fine."

She looked at my computer screen. Microsoft Word had been minimized. YouTube was up. There was a video of a lady with a big booty twerking.

"This is you writing?"

"Sometimes when I write I watch YouTube. It gives me inspiration. You know that."

"Right."

She walked off to the living room.

And I continued writing. But I didn't write about butts anymore. I started working on a list that I was planning on sending to Cracked.com.

The list was called: TOP FIVE SEXIEST TRANS-
FORMERS (AND YES GOBOTS COUNT, DON'T BE A
SNOB)

I could only think of a few Transformers. There was
Arcee. The pink lady from the movie. She was hot. Great
legs.

Then there was that chick from the GoBots but she kinda
seemed so cheap and tacky. I thought trannies were sexy. But
did I really want to open up about that in an article about female Transformers?

I was online researching female Transformers when Bella
came in again.

She looked at the screen and saw a picture of a Transform-
er.

"You have to be kidding me," she said.

I shut my laptop.

"It's not what you think," I said.

"This is fucked," she said.

She stormed off.

I chased after her.

She liked that.

Soon we were playing tag.

I caught her at one point and pulled her pants down and
smelled her butt.

Then I dragged her off to the bedroom.

We started having sex.

"Have you noticed our sex has gotten a lot more cuddly?"
I asked.
She nodded.
Then she kissed me.
Then I kissed her back.

YELLOW SNOWMEN

It was only thirty-two degrees but it felt so warm.

I took Bella on a hike. There was a trail off Route 38, about five minutes outside of Racine. It was usually used for dog walking.

Bella loved that. She loved dogs and she loved hiking. This trail combined both.

Every time we passed a family with their dog, we stopped. Bella would pet the dogs and tell them how cute they were.

It was a nice trail, but you had to walk slowly 'cause there was dog poop everywhere.

I was shocked by how far back the trail went. Soon we felt like we were alone.

We walked down near a stream. Parts of it were frozen, other parts were melting. It made nice sounds and colors.

I took a picture but it was blurry.

Then I saw Bella taking a piss on a tree. I took a picture of that and it was like the camera saw my wife's ass and woke up. The picture came out perfectly.

Bella caught me taking pictures of her butt and she got up, pulled her pants up and started chasing me.

She caught me and tickled me.

"Stop," I said. "We're hiking. This is very serious stuff we're doing."

She laughed.

We continued to march through the woods.

Occasionally we would see someone with a dog or a few dogs. They were usually small and looked desperate for attention. I felt bad for them. Being kept in some home, doing nothing but eating gross food and being fondled by your owners sounded awful.

There was this one dog though. He was big and black and he snarled at us. His owner apologized, but I liked that beast. It was scary.

"We need to find a new show," Bella said.

"No we don't. No more shows. All we do is watch shows."

"Come on. You love binge watching shows with me. You love to get all cuddly on the couch with me. You made us binge watch the fuck out of that show *Girls*."

"It's a good show. But I don't care. I hate how much time I spend watching all that shit. It's such a waste."

"Don't be so dramatic."

I kissed Bella on the forehead and grabbed her butt a little.

"You remember that weird kid we went to college with that lived in a teepee out in the woods?"

Bella rolled her eyes. She had big eyes.

"Didn't you date that kid?"

"NO! We hooked up like once."

"Was it romantic?" I asked.

"Shut up."

"That kid was kinda dumb."

"He was very dumb," she said. "But good at living in the woods though. That's for sure."

"Did he have a big dick?" I asked.

"Really big."

"HA! I CAUGHT YOU!" I yelled.

"What the fuck are you talking about?" she said.

"You once told me that his dick was small. And then you once told me that his dick was average. Do you just make this shit up as you go along?"

"I wasn't lying. Maybe I just got confused."

"Well, what about that kid Travis? The super dumb one with the ponytail."

"Are you serious right now?" she yelled.

"Come on. Consider this a scientific experiment."

"Oh yeah, you're really fucking scientific," she said in her mocking voice.

"Just tell me, was it big or not?"

"It was big," she said.

"HA! I was at that orgy. I had my face all in that Devon girl's butthole area, but I did get to see that kid naked and his dick was not big at all. It was average."

"It's bigger than yours," she said.

I tried to think of a snappy come back, but too much time passed, so I gave up on that.

"Touché," I said.

She made a snotty face at me.

"So did it smell good?" I asked.

"Did what smell good?"

"That kid's dick."

"What kid?"

"Teepee master."

"It smelled okay, I guess."

"More lies!" I yelled. "That guy lived in a fucking Teepee. In the middle of the fucking woods. In fucking Vermont. I guarantee his balls stank and I want to know what they smelled like."

"Does that turn you on?"

"A little."

"Does it get you all horny?" she asked.

She was using her sexy voice now. And I was getting a boner.

"Do you want to know what it tasted like?" she asked.

"Tell me what it was like, baby."

"Well, I don't remember so fuck off."

I laughed.

"Come on, how can you not remember what that hippy's dick smelled like?"

A mother and daughter walked by. They had a pug with them. The mother gave me a nasty look. So did the pug. The little girl looked oblivious.

Bella stopped.

Took a picture of a tree with some fog surrounding it.

She handed me the camera so I could see the picture. It was beautiful.

I asked her to take a picture of me.

I posed. I leaned on a tree and looked as thoughtful and at peace with nature as possible.

She took the picture.

I took the camera and looked at it.

"I look ridiculous," I said, feeling very self-conscious.

"Sorry 'bout that," she said.

"You take such good pictures of nature, but you take horrible pictures of me."

She pointed to an old barn in the distance.

"I wish I lived in a house like that," she said.

"Me too. One day."

She sighed.

"I bet Leonardo DiCaprio's penis smells really good," she said.

"I guarantee you it smells good," I said. "I bet he has the best dick in Hollywood."

"I wish I could see it. Just once."

"One day I'm sure there will be a movie with a shot of his dick in it."

"I sure hope so," she said.

CAGE FIGHTING

Winter had bested me.

I was acting even sloppier than usual.

Mount Dishberg was taller and more ominous than ever before.

My dirty laundry was like a slow moving tsunami.

My books were everywhere.

I was depressed.

I slept until noon.

I acted withdrawn and irritable.

And I suffered from rampant nostalgia.

I missed the messy rundown crankiness of Vermont.

Vermont was where Bella and I first met.

I missed mountains.

I missed the way rivers sounded in the early spring and the way they tasted in the late summer, early fall.

I missed Stewart's. I missed all the hicks that would line up outside and get drunk there at all hours of the day.

I missed hippy girls with armpit hair. Stinky armpit hair.

Bella grew her hair out for me but she wouldn't let herself get stinky.

I missed all things stinky.

I missed the stink of sweaty skin. And damp feet.

I missed the stink of dirty hair.

I missed the smell of bonfires.

Bella missed all that too. But that mutual nostalgia didn't bring us closer together.

We got into lots of fights. Even more than usual.

Bella and I liked to fight. We fought at least once a day.

But one night we got into a real bad fight.

We hadn't had this kind of fight in a long time.

It went on for hours.

We yelled and threw things.

We gave each other the silent treatment five times.

Bella stormed off and then stormed back into the bedroom ten times.

Finding a resolution seemed impossible.

She was a nag and mean during the fights so it was easy to blame things on her.

I threatened to leave.

But she called my bluff.

I couldn't leave.

I was too anxiety-ridden to be away from her.

I would only be punishing myself.

We kept fighting.

No resolution was found.

At times it felt like we were on the verge of resolution, but then it would all fall apart again.

I would start telling her how mean she could be.

She would get on me about my sloppiness.

"What if we had kids?" she said.

That was the first time she had brought that up.

I didn't know what to say.

I was not prepared for fatherhood.

"Would you expect me to work and then come home and clean and shit?" she said. "How can I expect you to take care of a baby if every time you get bummed out you let your whole world fall to shit?"

"I don't know," I said.

I started expressing my emotions by breathing heavily and cursing under my breath.

It made Bella feel bad. I could tell.

We continued fighting.

I told her I needed her to be more supportive, that I was in a funk.

"But you're already a slob when you're not in a funk. So when you get in a funk everything just gets too fucked up."

"That's a good point."

We continued fighting, but we had run out of steam.

We had fought to the point of exhaustion.

I got into bed.
We cuddled a bit.
Then I got up and took a shower.
When I got back to bed she was asleep.
I felt raw.
I didn't want to give myself into the dream world in this condition.

LETTERS

Bella came home early.

She had a half-day at work.

She was so happy and warm.

I kissed her face. Her forehead and her cheeks and her chin and her nose and her lips.

I asked her about work.

She smiled.

There was this one kid from her program that acted up a lot. He called her a fat bitch. He called her that a lot.

Recently he had gotten into kicking.

Sometimes he would try and write her notes. But they were illegible.

But they had taught him how to type. And he had written this letter.

Dear Bella

Rules for Kevin: no kicking, no saying "shut the fuck up." No hitting, not sticking up middle finger.
Kevin says "Sorry for kicking you and sticking up middle finger."
I love you Bella
From
Kevin.

THE ENDLESS FLESH

That night we went to my father's house and made him dinner.

My father loved Bella's quesadillas. He had been begging for her to make him some for months. So we made a batch, then drove them over to his place.

He was happy to see us.

We all sat in his living room and ate.

My father's nightgown didn't fit him well. It was too short. We could see his balls.

"Jesus, Bill," Bella said. "Put a tarp over that thing."

"A tarp?" I said.

And I laughed.

"Look at those things," I said. "They're even bigger than mine."

"Your old man has the best ball sack cleavage in all of

Wisconsin."

We laughed wildly.

"Can you two stop?" my dad said.

He acted annoyed but we could tell he was having a good time.

"There's so much flesh," Bella said.

"It looks like a storm cloud," I said. "It's like a bread bowl filled with clam chowder."

Bella laughed so hard she rolled off the couch.

Then she got up and started jumping up and down and doing little jump kicks.

My dad rolled his eyes. But in an affectionate way.

I continued talking about his balls.

"They look like the balls of T-Rex," I said. "They look like two dinosaur eggs. And you know what is inside of those eggs? Weird versions of me. It's like an alternate universe in there. There's like a million other versions of me, those big ass balls. I bet there's a version of me that's a doctor in there. And I bet there's a version of me that ended up being a time traveler. And I bet that time traveler has gone back in time so much. I bet he has gone back to the beginning of time and fucked the God that made time up and that she had big old God ass. So good."

"What are you talking about?" my dad asked.

"He's talking about your balls," Bella said.

"That's right. Your balls. Your big old dad balls. It looks like Epcot center down there. It looks like Mickey Mouse's ears. It looks like an elderly Winnie the Pooh. They look like a little pile of seaweed. They look like garlic knots. They look like the earth once looked when it was just a rock with some ocean on it. It looks like the space ship the Borg fly around in, only less cube-like and more saggy. Jesus, they are so big. I bet there are entire galaxies in those things. There's probably a version of me that's the Captain of a Star Ship and I bet that version of me is really responsible and remembers to do his space dishes. Look at those two giant balls. Look at all that flesh. It's chaotic under that nightgown. It's lawless. It's like the wild wild west."

Justin Grimbol moves around a lot and writes books. He went to college for while, then he stopped going to college. He works sometimes. He was raised by ministers. Certain hymns make him cry.

Other Atlatl Press Titles

Arafat Mountain by Mike Kleine

Drinking Until Morning by Justin Grimbol

Fuckness by Andersen Prunty

Thanks For Ruining My Life by C.V. Hunt

Mastodon Farm by Mike Kleine

They Had Goat Heads by D. Harlan Wilson

Death Metal Epic (Book One: The Inverted Katabasis)
by Dean Swinford

Losing the Light by Brian Cartwright

The Beard by Andersen Prunty

www.ingramcontent.com/pod-product-compliance
Lightning Source LLC
Chambersburg PA
CBHW061453210726
48287CB00007B/2492